For Jason, Nathan and Nichole,
and my loving husband, Ralph.
~R.W.

To Mam & Dad
Love
Robin Wimbiscus

Published by the Historical Pages Company
188 Main Street, Poultney, Vermont 05764
Visit us at: www.historicalpages.com

Text and illustrations © 1998 by Robin Wimbiscus
Book and cover design: Penny H. Sheehan

This book was typeset in Adobe Caslon.
The illustrations were done in colored pencil.

First U.S. edition 2006
ISBN 0-9772692-9-9

Printed by Journal Press, Inc., Poultney, Vermont

Somewhere in the Garden

Written
and
Illustrated
by
Robin
Wimbiscus

HISTORICAL PAGES COMPANY
188 Main Street, Poultney, Vermont 05764

Nichole and her mother had just finished marking all the flowers and vegetables in the garden with handmade tags made with cardboard, colored markers, popsicle sticks and pieces of bright yarn. "This way," her mother said. "Any time we need food or flowers from the garden, you'll be able to read the tags and easily find just what we need."

It was midday, and time for lunch. As they were leaving the garden, mother suddenly turned to Nichole, and said, "I must have left my favorite pen somewhere in the garden. Could you find it for me while I make our lunch?"

"Sure, mom," Nichole said with a beaming smile, as she looked out over the huge garden, wondering where to start. "I know where to begin," Nichole thought with delight as she went back into the garden. "I'll search from A to Z." Nichole knelt down and began her search by lifting up an oak-shaped leaf belonging to the...

Acorn Squash

shaped like a walnut shell, but dark green and ribbed from end to end, but no sign of the pen. Nichole continued her hunt for the pen by following the long vines of the squash until she was right under a teepee of…

a

Acorn squash

A a

Beans

climbing and covering the teepee of
tree branches her father had cut and
shaped for the beans to grow on.
Nichole was about to continue on,
when along came a hummingbird to
feed on the bright red flowers. Just
then, Nichole became hungry
herself. She grabbed a few beans
and continued to search under the…

b

Cucumbers

where the sharp spines covering the cucumbers' green bumpy skins reminded Nichole that she had to be very careful looking for the lost pen. "No pen here," Nichole said aloud, as she walked along the vines that were creeping and crawling their way over to the…

c

Dill

with its feather like leaves
tickling her nose as she knelt
to examine the ground.
The large flowery heads of dill
grew taller than Nichole, and cast
a shadow onto the…

d

Eggplant

so deep purple in color. As Nichole was thinking that the eggplant was the prettiest vegetable in the whole garden, her eyes spotted something long and thin.

"Yes, I found the pen," Nichole yelled with excitement. She reached under the drooping leaves of the eggplant and picked up…

Eggplant

E e

"A wiggling worm!" she cried in surprise. "I don't think mom would like you in our house," With a little giggle, she placed him gently back down in among the…

Fennel

that smelled so good she had to try a little piece. It looks a little like dill she thought, but it tastes like licorice candy. Looking around on the ground for the pen, she noticed that fennel has an edible bulb just like…

f

Garlic

a few feet away. The ivory white bulbs were made up of little pieces her mother called cloves. Nichole began to daydream about her mom's delicious warm garlic bread, when she remembered she had to find the pen. The next stop was nearby, and it was a dangerous one. Nichole was going to be extra careful looking under the…

Hot peppers

which are small, fiery-red and hot. There was no sign of the pen, so Nichole quickly made her way across the garden to the tall stalks of…

h

Indian corn

whose colorful cobs are full of
red, black, blue, yellow, even
orange kernels.
For all of her searching, Nichole
was already through the letter "I"
and still had not found the pen.
Her next stop would be easier, and
more fun to search, so she headed
in the direction of the big, orange…

i

Indian Corn

I i

Jack 0' Lanterns

the large round pumpkins, with scary faces. Nichole and her mother had already carved some pumpkins into Jack 0' Lanterns right there in the garden. When Nichole reached behind a scary Jack 0' Lantern, to move a small pumpkin in her way, her hands wrapped around something cold and round. But when she brought her hands out from under the large leaves, she was holding…

Jack-O-Lantern

J j

"A big fat toad!" Nichole laughed at her own mistake. "You weren't sitting on mom's pen." When she finally found a good, safe spot, Nichole carefully placed the toad in under the…

Kale

where the toad could hide under its curly purple-green leaves. Maybe the toad would lead me to the pen Nichole thought, so she waited quietly for a few minutes. Just then, the toad hopped into a patch of…

k

Kale

K k

Lettuce

with its sweet and tender leaves. Nichole followed the toad as she nibbled on a little red lettuce and then a little of the green. Continuing on, she walked almost all the way across the garden to search over near the fence by the…

Morning glories

where the warm sun had opened the trumpet-shaped flowers. No pen here either, and she was already halfway through the alphabet. Nichole smelled each flower as she followed their twisting vines over to the…

m

Nasturtiums

She searched among the bright red, yellow and orange flowers, when she suddenly noticed her nose was heading straight for a busy honey bee. She stopped herself quickly enough to avoid being stung and followed the black and yellow bee as it flew over to the…

n

Onions

Nasturtiums

N n

Onions

that were ready for harvest as they were popping out of the ground. Nichole followed the neatly planted rows until she found herself in a patch of…

o

Peas

that grew thick and tangled near the onions. As Nichole tugged on a plump green pod, looking forward to its crisp sweet peas, she saw something long and black by her feet. "Finally," Nichole cheered with a sigh, "the pen." As she bent down and lifted the sagging vine of peas she found…

p

"A Salamander!" Nichole laughed.
"Maybe you can help me find…,"
But before Nichole could finish
her sentence, the salamander ran
under the…

Queen Anne's Lace
which looked like soft snowflakes on a field of green grass. It reminded Nichole of winter. She thought about winter just long enough to let out a little shiver, then she wondered where the salamander had gone. Maybe, she thought, the salamander and the pen are both over by the…

Queen Ann's Lace

Q q

Radishes

which were crimson red and just beginning to grow out of the ground. "Nothing here," Nichole said to herself a little wearily, as she shook her head. She was very hungry now and thinking about giving up, when suddenly it occurred to her that she had not checked her favorite spot yet. As Nichole made her way down rows of plants she had already checked, she found herself dwarfed by her favorite plants in the whole garden…

r

Sunflowers

with their tall stems and large heart shaped leaves—they made a great fort for her to play in with her brothers. Even though the pen was nowhere in sight, the smile on Nichole's face was as big as the yellow flowers that followed the sun. Nichole was warmed by the sunflowers and continued to her next stop, the…

S

Sunflower

S s

Tomatoes

which were hanging red, ripe and heavy on their cages. Nichole could not resist such a tasty treat, and plucked a juicy tomato off the vine. As she bit into the tomato, the red juice dribbled down her chin onto a bouquet of…

t

Ursinias

whose dazzling yellow-orange petals were now splattered with red. Nichole was wiping her chin, when she noticed a butterfly resting nearby in the sunshine. As she put her hand out to pet its beautiful wings, the butterfly flew over to the…

u

Ursinia

U
u

Violas

dense patch of tiny yellow and purple flowers. When she saw the flowers, Nichole smiled. To her, they looked like a bunch of happy faces. She began to sing to the flowery faces, when she suddenly remembered her mother was counting on her to find the pen. She was still singing, when she reached the rows of…

v

Watermelons

Nichole knew the marbled green outer skin was hiding the sweet, pink juices inside, and couldn't wait to eat them. She really wished that the melons were also hiding the pen. Under the last leaf of the watermelon, she found a spider connecting its web to the…

W

Watermelon

W
W

Xeranthemums

with their stiff pointed flowers of pink and purple. Nichole ran through the alphabet in her mind, she was already at the letter "X" and realized she was running out of places to look for her mother's pen. Determined to find the pen, she turned around and headed right for the…

X

Yellow wax beans

which were hanging long and straight from their vine. Their thick leaves made it hard to see if the pen was hiding there. She took her time searching, and munching on fresh beans. "No pen," she said out loud. "One last place to look." She walked over to the edge of the garden, where she stood for a moment looking at the...

y

Yellow Wax Beans

Y y

Zucchini

hiding many long green squashes under its broad leaves. "Maybe it was hiding the pen as well," thought Nichole. Nichole lifted the last leaf…

Z

Zucchini

Zz

She heard her mother call. "Lunch is ready!" Nichole knew finding the pen wasn't a big deal, but felt sad as she began to walk slowly towards her mother.

"Come sit on the steps with me and have some lunch," said Mother cheerfully. "You must be hungry." Nichole realized she had tasted just about everything edible in the garden and had no room for lunch. Not wanting to hurt her mother's feelings she thought she would have a bite or two.

As Nichole went to sit down…

...She realized there was
something in her back pocket...

As the fog rises

I lay fast asleep

Not until the sun is high in the sky

Will I awake.

When consciousness becomes me

I make my routine journey to the garden.

There I indulge on the delicious green peas,

Fresh off the vine.

No better a breakfast anytime.

~ Nichole Wimbiscus, 1999